Bingo and th

M000210921

Story by Annette Smith
Illustrations by Pat Reynolds

Rigby®

A Harcourt Achieve Imprint

www.Rigby.com
1-800-531-5015

2

Mom and Sam and Bingo
went down to the river
for a walk.

"Look at the ducks," said Sam.

"Here they come."

The ducks looked at Bingo.

Bingo ran up to the ducks.

Woof! Woof! Woof!

"No, Bingo! No!" said Sam.

The ducks ran away.

Bingo ran after the ducks.

"**Bingo**," shouted Sam,

"come back here!"

The ducks ran down to the river.

Bingo ran down to the river, too.
Woof! Woof! Woof!

"Bingo! Bingo!" cried Sam.
"Come back here to me!"

"Bingo is in the water,"
said Sam.

Sam and Mom ran after Bingo.

"Come back, Bingo!"
shouted Sam.

"You are a **naughty** dog!"

Bingo looked up.

He came back to Sam.

"Good dog, Bingo," said Sam.

"You came back."